Fay
Goes to the Dance

First published in the United Kingdom in 2005
by Chrysalis Children's Books,
an imprint of Chrysalis Books Group plc
The Chrysalis Building
Bramley Road
London W10 6SP
www.chrysalisbooks.co.uk

This book was created for Chrysalis Children's Books by Zuza Books.
Text and illustrations copyright © Zuza Books

BRITISH LIBRARY CATALOGUING-IN-PUBLICATION DATA
A catalogue record for this book is available from the British Library.

ISBN 1 84458 579 4

Printed in China
2 4 6 8 10 9 7 5 3 1

Fay
Goes to
the Dance

Zuza Vrbova

Illustrated by Tom Morgan-Jones

CHRYSALIS CHILDREN'S BOOKS

It was the last day of the summer holidays.

Fay was listening to her favourite CD and
dancing around her bedroom.

As she was bouncing on her bed, her phone rang.
She leaped off the bed gracefully to answer it.

"Hi, Fay, it's Harriet," said the voice on the phone.
I am SO looking forward to seeing everyone
again tomorrow!"

"So am I!" said Fay, yelling above the music.
"I haven't seen anyone, apart from you, all summer."

The next morning, Fay had a spring in her step
as she headed to school. She saw Harriet, Roddy,
Bertie, Lucy and Lauren up ahead, so she ran
to catch up with them.

"Did everyone enjoy the holidays?" Fay asked.

"You bet!" said Roddy. "But I didn't grow as much as you did, Beanpole!"

Fay looked at her friends. They did seem to be much shorter than her now.

"Don't be so rude, Roddy!" Lucy snapped. "So what if Fay is taller? At least now she can reach the lovely juicy apples in those trees!"

At playtime, Connie, Leo and Tabby were skipping.

"Come and join in, Fay," called Tabby.

But when Fay started skipping, the rope kept bumping into her head.

"Fay, get your head out of the way," Connie said.

"I can't lift the rope high enough,"
Tabby added in a huff.

"I'm sorry," Fay said sadly.

"I guess I'm just too tall to skip."

9

After playtime, Miss Roo made an announcement.

"We're going to start dance classes!" she said.

A few people groaned, but Fay was happy.

She loved dancing and she was good at it.

"Right, let's go to the gym and get started!"

Miss Roo said smiling.

11

In the gym, Miss Roo said,

"OK, everyone find a partner."

   The class shuffled around,

looking for someone to dance with.

Fay thought she might like to dance with Marcus, but he had already paired up with Tabby. So Fay went to look for George. But he had paired up with Beryl.

Nobody wants to dance with me because I'm too tall, Fay thought.

Miss Roo took Fay's hand. "Don't worry, Fay," she said. "I'll be your partner."

Fay didn't want to be different and she certainly didn't want to dance with Miss Roo.

Miss Roo showed everyone the steps. Then she put on a CD so that everyone could try dancing in time to the music.

Miss Roo didn't pay attention to Fay at all. She was too busy looking around at everyone else.

15

Fay began to dread dance class. The next week,
just like before, Miss Roo asked everyone to find
a dance partner. The class rushed around to pair up,
but Fay just stood still.

No one wants to dance with a giant,
she thought.

Then she heard Roddy's voice in her ear.

"I think I'll pair up with you," he said.
"Then I can stamp on your toes, Long Legs!"

Fay did not want to dance with Roddy,
but she had no choice. Everyone else had
already found a partner.

Fay started to hate going to school.

   I am the tallest person in the class, Fay thought as she stood in the queue in the canteen. And being taller than everyone else makes me different.

She tried to make herself shorter by stooping,
but it didn't work. She was still much taller than
all her friends. And stooping made her back hurt.

    I wish I wasn't a beanpole, Fay thought.

Fay stopped skipping with her friends
at playtime. She didn't like climbing
on the climbing frame anymore either.
It just made her feel even taller.

Instead, she played on her own
with her hula-hoop. And she tried hard
to ignore Roddy when he called her
"Beanpole" or "Long Legs".

21

One morning, Miss Roo announced,

"There's going to be a school dance next week.

You can all show off your dance moves!"

Oh no! Fay thought. I REALLY don't want
to go to the dance.

Martha was sitting next to Fay.
"I'm not going," she said firmly.

"Why not?" asked Fay, a bit surprised.

"No one ever wants to dance with me.
I'm just too small," Martha replied.

"Well, no one ever wants to dance with me because I'm too tall," said Fay.

They looked at each other in amazement. They both felt the same!

"Well, perhaps we could go, but just not dance with anyone," suggested Fay.

"It's a deal!" replied Martha.

Fay and Martha decided to make outfits for the dance.

"Don't forget our deal," Fay said, sticking some
yellow stars onto her ra-ra skirt. "No dancing!"

"No dancing," promised Martha.

At the dance, Fay and Martha sat next to each other, tapping their feet in time to the music.

George went up to Fay. "Would you like to dance with me?" he asked politely.

"No, thank you, George," said Fay, winking at Martha. George walked away, looking a bit sad.

Then Harriet went up to Martha. "Hey, Martha, would you like to dance?" she asked.

"Sure!" Martha replied and jumped off her chair.

"But what about our deal?" said Fay.

"Maybe the deal wasn't such a good idea. We're here now, so let's have a dance!" Martha said, trying to pull Fay off her chair.

But Fay didn't move. "I always stick to my promises," she said.

Fay sat by herself and watched everyone else dance.

Martha seems to be having fun, even though she's small, Fay thought.

Then Fay watched Roddy stomping about. He was having fun too.

And she saw Crispin enjoying himself as usual. Crispin couldn't dance at all (he kept falling over), but he didn't seem to care.

In fact, no one seems to care what anyone else thinks. They're all just having a good time, she thought.

At that moment, Fay's favourite song came on.

Before she knew it, she had leaped out of her chair.

I don't care what anyone thinks either, she thought.

I'm going to dance to my favourite song!

So Fay held her head up high and danced and danced.

She loved every minute of it and she was fantastic.

Everyone watched Fay and clapped and cheered.

Maybe it doesn't matter if I'm tall, thought Fay.

And anyway, the others still have a long way to grow!

Top of the Class

Collect them all!

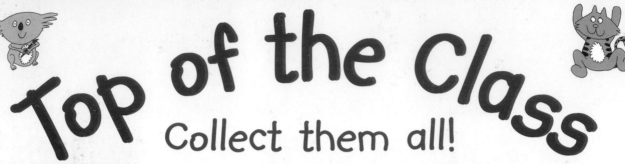

Ellie Takes a Chance — Zuza Vrbova, Illustrated by Tom Morgan-Jones — 1-84458-483-6

Zoë Wins the Race — Zuza Vrbova, Illustrated by Tom Morgan-Jones — 1-84458-407-0

Piers Finds his Voice — Zuza Vrbova, Illustrated by Tom Morgan-Jones — 1-84458-406-2

George Makes Friends — Zuza Vrbova, Illustrated by Tom Morgan-Jones — 1-84458-482-8

Lisa Comes to the Rescue — Zuza Vrbova, Illustrated by Tom Morgan-Jones — 1-84458-578-6

Tabby Saves the Day — Zuza Vrbova, Illustrated by Tom Morgan-Jones — 1-84458-481-X

Kit Paints the Sky — Zuza Vrbova, Illustrated by Tom Morgan-Jones — 1-84458-404-6

Leo Takes to the Stage — Zuza Vrbova, Illustrated by Tom Morgan-Jones — 1-84458-405-4

Roddy Learns a Lesson — Zuza Vrbova, Illustrated by Tom Morgan-Jones — 1-84458-480-1

Fay Goes to the Dance — Zuza Vrbova, Illustrated by Tom Morgan-Jones — 1-84458-579-4

Visit the Top of the Class website at
www.topoftheclassbooks.com